P9-CJS-287

Learning to Read, Step by Step!

 Ready to Read Preschool–Kindergarten
• big type and easy words • rhyme and rhythm • picture clues
For children who know the alphabet and are eager to begin reading.

 Reading with Help Preschool–Grade 1
• basic vocabulary • short sentences • simple stories
For children who recognize familiar words and sound out new words with help.

 Reading on Your Own Grades 1–3
• engaging characters • easy-to-follow plots • popular topics
For children who are ready to read on their own.

 Reading Paragraphs Grades 2–3
• challenging vocabulary • short paragraphs • exciting stories
For newly independent readers who read simple sentences with confidence.

 Ready for Chapters Grades 2–4
• chapters • longer paragraphs • full-color art
For children who want to take the plunge into chapter books but still like colorful pictures.

STEP INTO READING® is designed to give every child a successful reading experience. The grade levels are only guides. Children can progress through the steps at their own speed, developing confidence in their reading, no matter what their grade.

Remember, a lifetime love of reading starts with a single step!

This book is for Shelby
—A.J.H.

Text copyright © 2003 by Anna Jane Hays. Illustrations copyright © 2003 by Valeria Petrone.
All rights reserved under International and Pan-American Copyright Conventions. Published in
the United States by Random House Children's Books, a division of Random House, Inc., New
York, and simultaneously in Canada by Random House of Canada Limited, Toronto.

www.randomhouse.com/kids

Library of Congress Cataloging-in-Publication Data
Hays, Anna Jane. The pup speaks up / by Anna Jane Hays ; illustrated by Valeria Petrone —
1st ed.   p.   cm. — (Step into reading.) "Step 1 book."
SUMMARY: After Bo and Pal, his silent new puppy, go for a walk and hear the various sounds of
animals and objects around them, Pal finally speaks up.
ISBN 0-375-81232-6 (trade) — ISBN 0-375-91232-0 (lib. bdg.)
[1. Animal sounds—Fiction. 2. Sound—Fiction. 3. Dogs—Fiction. 4. Pets—Fiction. 5. Animals—
Fiction.] I. Petrone, Valeria, ill. II. Title. III. Series. PZ7.H314917 Pu 2003 [E]—dc21
2002004585

Printed in the United States of America   17 16 15 14 13   First Edition

STEP INTO READING, RANDOM HOUSE, and the Random House colophon are registered trademarks of
Random House, Inc.

The Pup Speaks Up

A Phonics Reader

by Anna Jane Hays
illustrated by Valeria Petrone

Random House 🏠 New York

Bo has a new pal.

Happy day!

5

"Hello!" says Bo.

"What do you say?"

6

The pup just wags
his tail.

Bo and Pal
go for a walk.
"What do you say?"
Bo asks a duck.

"Quack," says the duck.

"Honk," goes a truck.

9

"What do you say?"

Bo asks a bee.

"Buzz," says the bee.

"Buzz like me."

"Tick tock,"
goes a clock.

"Chug, chug,"

goes a tug.

A train calls,

"Choo choo!"

A baby cries,

"Boo-hoo!"

15

A rooster crows,

"Cock-a-doodle-do!"

An owl hoots,

"Hoo hoo! Hoo hoo!"

"What do you say?"

Bo asks Pal.

Pal just runs

and chases his tail.

A chick says,

"Cheep."

"Baa, baa,"

says a sheep.

19

A happy pig says,

"Oink, oink, oink."

boink

boink

boink

A bouncy ball goes

boink, boink, boink.

21

"Ribbit," says a frog.

But not the dog.

23

"What do you say?"

Bo asks his pup.

This time Pal
just jumps up.

"Moo!" says a cow.

Look out now . . .

Here comes a cat!

It says,

"MEOW!"

The pup speaks up!
"BOW WOW WOW!"

29

Bo says, "WOW!"

Hooray!

What a happy day!

31901059278004